Winter Shoes for Shadow Horse

by
Linda Oatman High

Illustrated by
Ted Lewin

Boyds Mills Press

With thanks to Glenn Hurst, Ammon Zimmerman,
and other farriers of Lancaster County
—L. O. H.

To Mike Dooling
—T. L.

U.S. Cataloging-in-Publication Data
   (Library of Congress Standards)

High, Linda Oatman.
   Winter shoes for shadow horse / by Linda Oatman High ;
illustrated by Ted Lewin. — 1st ed.
   [32] p. : col. ill. ; cm.
Summary: A boy shoes his first horse under the guidance of his father.
ISBN 1-56397-472-X
1. Horses — Fiction . 2. Fathers and sons — Fiction. I. Lewin, Ted. II. Title.
   [E]   21 2001 CIP   AC
00-107758

Text copyright © 2001 by Linda Oatman High
Illustrations copyright © 2001 by Ted Lewin
All rights reserved

Published by Caroline House
Boyds Mills Press, Inc.
A Highlights Company
815 Church Street
Honesdale, Pennsylvania 18431
Printed in China

First edition, 2001
The text of this book is set in 15-point Minion.

10 9 8 7 6 5 4 3 2 1

The nighttime glow of Papa's forge
and the ringing rhythm of his hammer
pull me through the dark
and into the blacksmith shop.

Blacksmithing   Welding
Horseshoeing   &   Woodwork

I stand by the door,
soaking up the warmth
and smelling the red-hot iron.

Papa works
and whistles
and watches the flame
as I watch him
and wonder when it will be my turn to learn
how to shoe a horse.

Finally,
Papa turns and looks at me.
"Winter shoes," he says.
"Snowstorm in the air."
I shiver and move closer to the fire,
handing Papa his box of tools.
"Ice nails," Papa says,
plucking a sharp-pointed nail from the pile.
"So the horses don't slip on the snow."

I nod,
and Papa goes to the window.
"Here comes Shadow Horse," he says.
The door blasts open with a whip of cold air,
and Mister Spencer leads Shadow Horse into the room.

Shadow Horse stomps
and snorts
and whinnies,
his brown eyes flashing with fear.
"Shadow Horse," I whisper,
stroking his silky face
and slipping him some brown sugar
from Papa's treat box.
Shadow Horse snuffles the sugar,
swishing his tail,
and Papa pats his back.

"Left foot first," Papa says,
leaning one hand
on Shadow Horse's shoulder
and gently pressing the horse
toward the right.
Shadow Horse lifts his left foot,
and Papa pulls pincers from his pocket.
Slowly,
Papa pries the old shoe
from Shadow Horse's hoof.

"Good horse," Papa whispers,
dabbing the hoof with melted pork fat salve.
He grabs his rasp and nippers
and trims Shadow Horse's hoof,
whistling all the while.

I fetch a shoe and some ice nails.
"Winter shoes for Shadow Horse," I say.
Tapping the nails with steady strokes,
Papa hammers on the horseshoe.
"A nip, a rasp, a clinch," he says,
teaching me.
"One shoe on, three to go."

Two shoes later,
Papa looks at me.
"Your turn," he says,
and I go cold as snow.
I take the tools and apron, shaking,
hoping to please Papa.
"What if he kicks me?" I ask.
"He won't," says Papa.
"What if I hurt him?" I ask.
"You won't," Papa says, and smiles.
I take a deep breath,
and then I work.

I pry,
and salve,
and whisper,
and tap
and nip and rasp and clinch,
Papa's hand on my shoulder.
Shadow Horse's back ripples and I flinch, scared.
"Go on," Papa whispers,
his hand heavy and strong.

Finally,
it's finished:
Shadow Horse has winter shoes.
I stand, glad the job is over,
and Papa presses the old shoe into my hand.
"A first horseshoe," he says,
"is to be saved for always."
I hold the horseshoe tight.

We all go through the doorway and into the night.
Leading Shadow Horse in a slow circle,
Papa watches his gait and nods.
"He's good for the winter," he calls out.

Mister Spencer climbs onto Shadow Horse's back,
as Papa and I watch
from the doorway.
Shadow Horse canters away,
winter shoes pounding the ground.

My heart hammering with the sound,
I lift the horseshoe high and wave good-bye.
Papa and I listen
as Shadow Horse and his winter shoes
melt away into blackness.
"Snow is in the air," Papa says.
"More horses will need winter shoes."

And then we turn and walk,
together,
back into the blacksmith shop.